Kitten In A Box

Inspirited by Wanda,
For Anya and Dalton,
With a heart full of gratitude to Nino-

Kitten In A Box

ISBN: 9798588191791

Printed in the United States of America

Kitten, kitten,
Kitten In A Box

Kitten in a Toy box,

A music box,

A shoe box,

An old box,
A new box,
Kitten in a
Blue box.

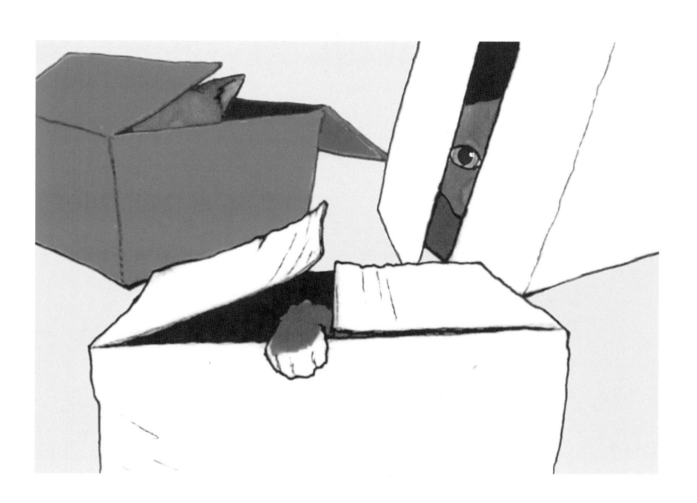

Is this a box?

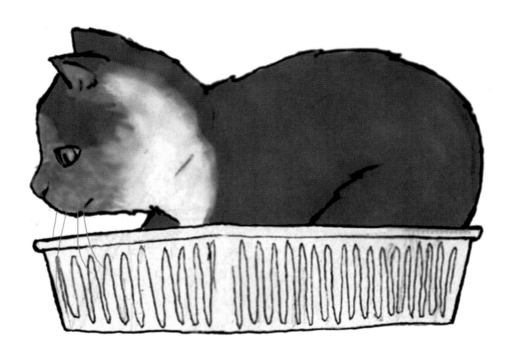

Kitten, kitten,
Kitten In A Box

A box of rocks,

A planter box,

Whiskers,
Nose
And tippy-toes
Peeking through a
Tissue box.

Kitten, kitten,
Kitten In A Box

Kitten in a bowl,

Kitten,
Roll, roll, roll

Under blankets,

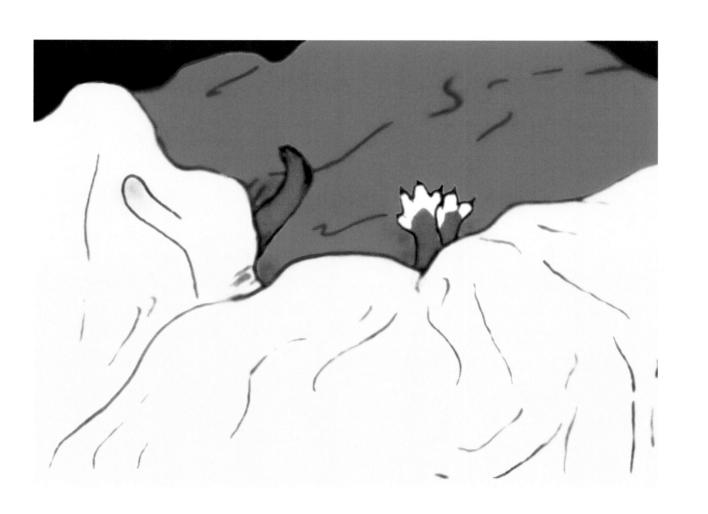

In the socks,

And then
She hides,

Under a box!

Kitten, kitten,
Kitten In A Box

Kitten in a pan,
Under Blankets
On some rocks,

But the favorite Place of all, Is

Kitten In A Box

MY FAVORITE KITTY

Created By

_____

My favorite kitty's name is,

_____

Here's a drawing of my cat.

My kitty plays like this,

And my kitty hides like that.

My kitty does some silly things at times,
As you can see,

But my favorite time is kitty snuggling close to me.

The End

Made in the USA
Columbia, SC
05 February 2021